ABOUT THIS BOOK

The collaboration between Mumsnet, Gransnet and Walker Books to find talented new voices has become an incredibly popular annual competition. Hundreds of hopeful authors entered their animal stories and the ten winning entries were chosen by a panel of celebrity judges, chaired by former Children's Laureate Anthony Browne. The stories were illustrated by upcoming artists as part of a collaborative process. The result is a beautiful treasury which proudly showcases new talent.

First published 2014 by Walker Books Ltd

87 Vauxhall Walk, London SE11 5HJ

10 9 8 7 6 5 4 3 2 1

Text © 2014 Mumsnet Limited

Illustrations: "Little Miss Wolfy Good" © 2014 Mel Howells; "Captain Yuri and the Space Mission" © 2014 Fiona Ross; "The Hedgehog Who Wouldn't Sleep" © 2014 Narisa Togo; "The Great Meerkat Escape" © 2014 Hannah Beech; "The Tale of the Winged Lion" © 2014 Kate Alizadeh; "The Elephant Carnival" © 2014 Briony May Smith; "A Pile of Panda" © 2014 Rachel Stubbs; "Atuki and Serai" © 2014 Martha Anne; "Up In the Trees Is Not For Me!" © 2014 Faye Bradley; "Basil the Brave" © 2014 Emma Collins

This book has been typeset in Cochin

Printed in China

British Library Cataloguing in Publication Data: a catalogue record for this book is available from the British Library

ISBN 978-1-4063-5790-5

www.walker.co.uk

WALKER BOOKS
AND SUBSIDIARIES
LONDON · BOSTON · SYDNEY · AUCKLAND

the **mumsnet** book of Animal Stories

TEN PRIZE-WINNING STORIES FROM MUMSNET & GRANSNET

FOREWORD

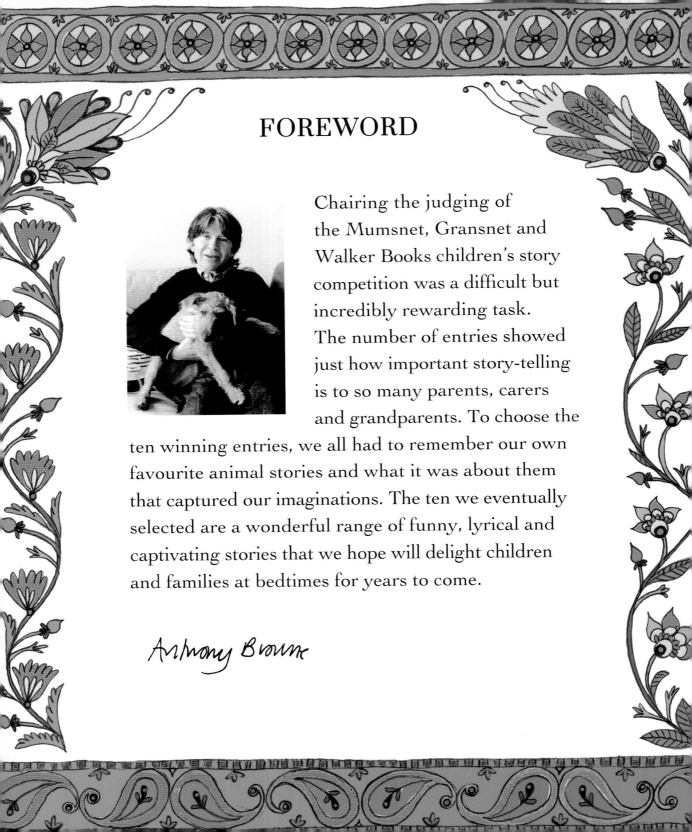

Chairing the judging of the Mumsnet, Gransnet and Walker Books children's story competition was a difficult but incredibly rewarding task. The number of entries showed just how important story-telling is to so many parents, carers and grandparents. To choose the ten winning entries, we all had to remember our own favourite animal stories and what it was about them that captured our imaginations. The ten we eventually selected are a wonderful range of funny, lyrical and captivating stories that we hope will delight children and families at bedtimes for years to come.

Anthony Browne

CONTENTS

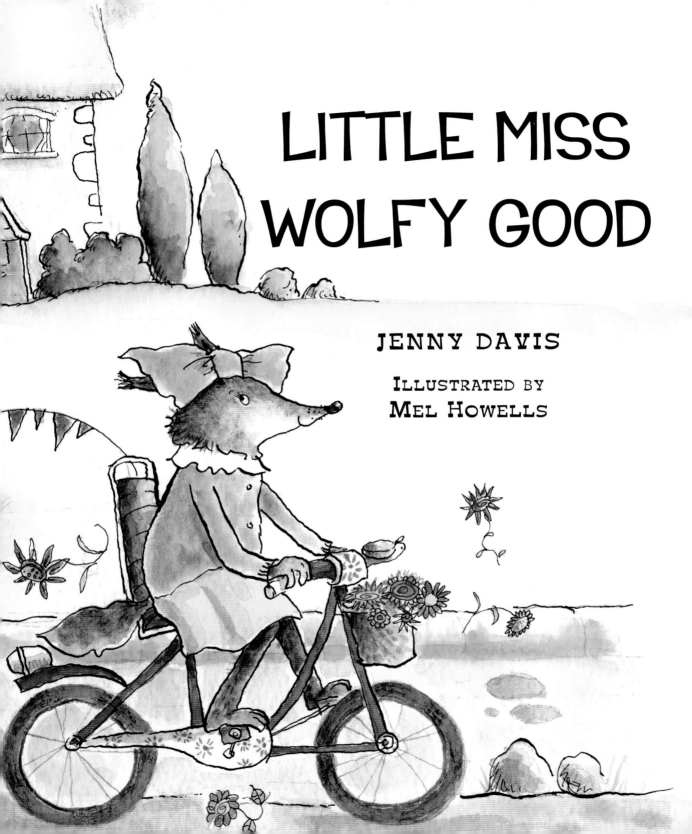

LITTLE MISS WOLFY GOOD

JENNY DAVIS

ILLUSTRATED BY
MEL HOWELLS

Little Miss Wolfy Good was, as her name suggested, a very, very good wolf. She was so good she wasn't actually much like a wolf at all. She was more like a sweet pet poodle. Her fur was always tidy and she never went out without wearing her favourite pink bow. She was polite to everyone she met and spent most of her time helping others. Little Miss Wolfy Good was a very good wolf indeed.

On this particular morning, Little Miss Wolfy Good was just putting some freshly baked cookies in her basket to take to the old folk in the village when she heard a letter drop on her doormat. She opened it excitedly.

Dear Little Miss Wolfy Good,

Congratulations! You have been offered a place at Professor Huffanpuff's Academy for Big, Bad Wolves. We look forward to seeing you for your first lesson this morning.

Big, bad regards,
Mr Huffanpuff
Headmaster

"There must be some mistake," she said, smiling – because of course good wolves never, ever get cross. "I can't possibly go to a school for Big, Bad Wolves. I'm a good wolf. I'll pop into the Academy and explain that they must have muddled me up with someone else." She straightened her bow, picked up the basket of cookies and left.

Little Miss Wolfy Good skipped all the way to the Academy for Big, Bad Wolves. It had a huge, dirty front door. Little Miss Wolfy Good knocked gently and wondered if she had time to wipe her grubby paw on a tissue. But the door slowly opened and a rather large, grumpy-looking wolf boomed,
"Hello, Little Miss Wolfy Good! We've been expecting you. Come this way."

Little Miss Wolfy Good was far too polite to interrupt him. She stepped through the door and followed him to a small classroom. Inside were lots of wolves dressed up in clothes a sweet old lady might wear.

"Your first lesson is on how to trick Red Riding Hood. You must make her believe you are Grandma," said the grumpy wolf.

Little Miss Wolfy Good thought this was a good time to leave. She didn't want to trick anyone, especially not a nice little girl doing a good deed. In her most polite voice she said, "I'm sorry, there must be some mistake. I really shouldn't be here, I'm far too good."

But she was so quiet that nobody heard her. Soon she was dressed in a frilly nightgown and cap and was sitting down with a group of bad-looking wolves. Little Miss Wolfy Good then had to practise all sorts of strange things.

The first was to try and drink tea like Grandma. She found this easy as she always drank her tea beautifully. However, the other wolves found it difficult and soon tea was flying everywhere. Little Miss Wolfy Good's nightgown was quickly splattered.

Then she had to practise talking like Grandma. She was good at this. But she was amazed at how all the other wolves struggled. None of them sounded like a kind old lady.

Little Miss Wolfy Good also had to practise catching Red Riding Hood and pretend to gobble her up. She found this much harder. She was far too lovely to try and catch anyone, and she didn't like eating little girls at all. She much preferred a slice of cake.

When the lesson was over, Little Miss Wolfy Good tried to make her way out of the classroom. But the other wolves were much bigger and she was caught in the middle of them with no way out.

She found herself in a new classroom, with lots of little houses made out of straw, sticks and bricks. Mr Huffanpuff was teaching this class. Little Miss Wolfy Good squeezed her way towards him, sure this time she would be able to explain about the mix-up.

In her sweetest voice she said, "I'm sorry, there must be some mistake. I really shouldn't be here, I'm far too good."

Mr Huffanpuff didn't hear her sweet voice. Instead he asked her to blow down the straw house. Little Miss Wolfy Good was far too polite to refuse and gave a little blow. But the house didn't move. She was much too gentle to blow a house down, even one made of straw.

Mr Huffanpuff was disappointed and made her practise at the front of the class for hours. Little Miss Wolfy Good started to feel hot and tired. The other wolves had very bad breath and all the huffing and puffing had made the room smell.

Then Mr Huffanpuff announced that their final lesson was to chase the Three Little Pigs around the playing field.

"Oh no," thought Little Miss Wolfy Good. "I really must get out of here. I don't want to chase the Three Little Pigs. I don't even like running. Skipping is so much nicer!"

But before she knew it, she was caught up in a crowd of wolves, all running as fast as they could. By the time they had finished she was covered in mud, her pretty ribbon had fallen out and she was very sore and bruised.

Little Miss Wolfy Good was trying her hardest to smile when Mr Huffanpuff started handing out prizes for the baddest wolves.

"Thank goodness," she thought. "It's nearly over!"

"The prize for chasing the Three Little Pigs goes to Mr Speedy Wolf. Well done!" said Mr Huffanpuff. "And the prize for the best impression of Grandma goes to Little Miss Wolfy Good."

Little Miss Wolfy Good started to make her way to the front.

"At last!" she thought. "I can just get my prize and then I will never, ever come back!"

"Well done, Little Miss Wolfy Good," said Mr Huffanpuff. "You really do make a very sweet old lady. But you have to work much harder at scaring, chasing, huffing and puffing. We'll expect you back tomorrow and for the rest of the year, so we can make you the best bad wolf you can be."

Little Miss Wolfy Good couldn't stand it any longer. She began to breathe very deeply. She started huffing and puffing uncontrollably, louder and louder and louder, until she let out the most enormous *howl*.

"I'M FAR TOO GOOD TO BE HERE! YOU AND YOUR UGLY, SMELLY, DIRTY FRIENDS CAN KEEP YOUR LESSONS. I AM NOT INTERESTED!"

And at that moment, Little Miss Wolfy Good enjoyed being angry.

There was silence and then all of the other wolves started to cheer.

"That's more like it!" shouted Mr Huffanpuff.

Little Miss Wolfy Good never took the basket of cookies to the old folk that day. Instead she gobbled them all up herself. And from that day on, she was different. She was still very good, just very good at being very bad.

- CAPTAIN YURI -

AND THE
SPACE MISSION

SUSANNAH O'BRIEN

ILLUSTRATED BY **FIONA ROSS**

You can always tell when my owner, Arthur, has had a bad day at school because he comes running over to me the second he gets home.

"HAMISH, HAMISH, HAMISH!" he shouts, even though there's nothing wrong with my hearing. Then he opens the latch and reaches his big, mucky hands into my cage.

"My lovely little hamster, Haaaaamish!" he announces to the empty room. I always play a bit shy, but actually I don't mind. After a day stuck by myself, I'm quite glad of the company. But I don't want Arthur to know. He'll get a big head and think he's the bee's knees.

Mind you, he does treat me like a guinea pig sometimes. I am a hamster, for goodness' sake! I'm not here to be experimented on. It took me weeks to feel dry again after the time we went deep-sea diving in the bath.

Today, Arthur must have had a good day because he didn't come straight over to me. I could hear him chatting away to his mum and that sister of his in the kitchen. Arthur was talking about school. I thought it sounded boring. You had to stay in the same room all day with the same people and do as the teacher said. Arthur often complained that he wasn't allowed to play at school. I'm far too busy for playing. I've got this special wheel that I go round and round and round on all the time, and I'm busy running in it day and night. If a teacher started telling me what I could and couldn't do I'd get in a right old huff.

Anyway, after what must have been hours and hours, the phone rang and Arthur's mum went to answer it. I could hear Lucy and Arthur squabbling a bit more and then I heard Lucy storm up the stairs. That was when Arthur finally remembered his loyal hamster friend and came to see me at long last.

"Hamish, my boy Hamish!" He grabbed at me enthusiastically, but I was pretty cross with him for ignoring me, so I looked the other way. Then I pretended to be asleep. He was still really excited and jabbering away about his day, but he hadn't even said sorry for ignoring me. So I weed on him! That got his attention.

Eventually, after he had washed his hands, he came over to me again. We were both sorry and had a proper chat this time. I sat on his hand and he told me about his day.

"We had an amazing assembly today, Hamish. Amazing. It was about space. Do you know what space is?" He looked at me and waited for me to answer, but I chose not to. I did know a little about space, of course (sometimes it comes up on cartoons we watch together).

"Space is this really, really cool thing up in the sky, where all the planets are. Sometimes people go up to space!" Then Arthur pretended I was a rocket and he *whooshed* me into space. It was actually pretty good fun, until he did it a few too many times and I started to feel sick. I wondered what he was planning.

"I've decided that I want to go into space when I'm older," he said.

Now this was definitely interesting. Arthur and I stick together (I even had to go with him to his grandma's at Christmas). If he was going up into space, then I supposed I would go too.

The next day, Arthur came straight over to me, but this time he wasn't alone.

WHOOSH!

WHIZZZ!

"Good news, Hamish," he said when he reached me. He was speaking in that little show-offy voice he uses when he has a friend over for tea. "Dad said that I won't be able to get to space until I'm really old and I've finished school." That's a relief, I thought. "But me and Ted have come up with a plan," said Arthur.

Oh dear.

Ted grinned at me sheepishly from behind his fringe. He was very little, but he seemed like a nice boy. He didn't ignore me when he came over. I must have looked quizzical, because Arthur picked me up carefully and held me close.

"Don't worry, the new plan is great. You're going to love it. First of all we're going to rename you. Your new name is Yuri."

Well! I wasn't best pleased, I can tell you. I'm not a baby for goodness' sake. You can't just suddenly change my name.

"We're naming you after Yuri Gagarin, the first man who ever went into space," Ted explained.

For the next hour or two, Arthur and Ted worked quietly at the dining table. I stayed in my cage. Arthur and I had been on plenty of adventures before, but this was looking different. Every so often one of them would come over for a quick chat or to show me something. From where I was standing, I could just about make out what was on the table. I saw lots of empty loo rolls and an egg box. There was some sticky tape and some glue, along with two big pairs of plastic scissors. After a little while, Arthur's mum came in with an old cereal box which they were both very excited about. Lucy came in for a bit to laugh at them, but they just ignored her. Then she said they could use her special paints if they wanted to. I could see that she was getting quite excited as well.

I began to panic. What exactly did Arthur have in mind?

After they had their dinner, they came back in to see me. Things seemed to be very serious all of a sudden.

"Yuri," Arthur said. "Yuri Hamish Hamster Jones, we are very pleased to tell you that you have been chosen for a very special project."

I groaned inwardly.

"YOU'RE GOING INTO SPACE, YOU'RE GOING INTO SPACE!" shouted Ted.

"TE-ED!" Lucy and Arthur were both cross with him for giving away the secret. I wasn't sure how I felt.

Then Ted brought over their afternoon's creation. It was a wobbly red cardboard rocket.

"Don't worry," said Lucy, "we've made it nice and comfy for you. There's a bit of straw and some of your food in there."

I wished I shared their confidence. Where would I end up? What would I find there?

They took me out into the garden to launch their mission. They put the cardboard rocket down on the grass (luckily it hadn't been raining), placed me in it and wished me luck.

I'll need more than luck, I thought.

"We can't wait to hear what it's like up there!" said Ted.

"I'm going to miss you, but I'll see you soon. You are being so brave!" said Arthur.

Then Lucy counted to three and they all said: "Brave astronaut of the Hamster Space Programme, we salute you!"

Then the countdown began.

"5!   4!   3!   2!   1!"

"BLAST OFF!"

Here we go! Let's hope aliens don't eat hamsters.

28

THE HEDGEHOG
WHO WOULDN'T SLEEP

ALISON WEBB

ILLUSTRATED BY
NARISA TOGO

Deep in the forest, as the days became shorter and
the nights grew longer, Little Spike and his mother
curled up inside a hollow tree stump on their nest of
pine needles and autumn leaves. Mother Hedgehog
turned to her son wearily. "Now it is time for us to sleep."

"But I'm not tired. I'm big and brave. Why can't
I stay up to see the winter?" the little hoglet protested.

Mother yawned, "You have much to learn.
Winter is no place for a hedgehog. The freezing north
wind whistles, the river turns to solid ice and our food
is buried beneath a carpet of snow. Now, snuggle up
and go to s … s … s … s…"

But Little Spike was not the least bit sleepy. He poked his snout out into the chilly air, then one paw, then another and then his entire bristly little body. He scampered off through the woodland, leaving his mother behind.

"I will just stay up for a short while," he thought. "After all, I am big and brave."

Then the excited hedgehog was stopped in his tracks by a squirrel, flashing his fluffy tail as he scurried along.

"Out of my way! Can't you see I am busy stashing nuts for the winter? You should be asleep by now!"

"Oh no, not me! I'm big and brave and I'm staying up to see the winter!" replied Little Spike.

"You really are a foolish little hoglet. Don't you know that the freezing north wind will soon be here, whistling its winter tune and making the leaves dance in its icy path?"

"A wind that whistles a tune?" thought Little Spike. "I would like to hear that!" And he scuttled on his way.

Soon he came to the river. A beaver
was gnawing through some branches.

"Out of my way! Can't you see that I am busy building
my lodge for the winter? It's far too late for you to be out."

"Oh no, not me! I'm big and brave and I'm staying
up to see the winter!" replied Little Spike.

"You really are a foolish little hoglet.
Don't you know that this river will soon
be frozen solid? There will be no
water to drink and you will
be slipping, sliding and
skating all over the place."

"Ice-skating?" thought
Little Spike. "I would
like to do that!" And he
trotted on his way.

The swooping swallows
were gathering in the grey sky.
"Out of our way!" they squawked,
as they flew over Little Spike's head.
"Can't you see that we are getting ready to
fly to the warm lands? You should be tucked
up in your nest."

"Oh no, not me! I'm big and brave and I'm
staying up to see the winter!" replied Little Spike.

"You really are a foolish little hoglet. Don't you
know that the snow will soon be here, burying your
food beneath a soft white freezing carpet?"

"A soft white carpet?" thought Little Spike.

"I would like to see that!" And he scurried
on his way.

As the small hedgehog went further and further from his nest, he didn't notice the sun setting in the darkening sky. The wind whistled and howled eerily through the trees. Leaves danced in circles across his path and he couldn't see his way. The icy cold wind hurt his nose and chilly tingles ran all the way down to his tiny paws.

"I don't like this north wind!" he thought, and he hurried on his way.

A strong gust blew Little Spike back to the riverbank. The river had turned to solid ice. The adventurous hedgehog placed one paw onto the ice, followed by a second, and then *wheee*…! He slipped and slid, skidded and he skated until he landed with a thud against a rock.

"I don't like this frozen river!" he thought, and he struggled on his way.

A single sparkling snowflake drifted from the dark sky and landed on Little Spike's snout. More and more snowflakes silently followed. The woodland was soon covered by a glistening white carpet.

Making tiny paw-prints in the fresh snow, the little hoglet began to trudge home. He was soon lost in the deepening drifts. He sniffed and scratched at the hard ground, looking for food.

As he climbed to the top of the hill, he smelt the cold air and tried to find his way. As far as his eyes could see, the whole world was still and white.

"I don't like this freezing white carpet!" he thought, and he huffed on his way.

Through the flurries, Little Spike could just make out a black-and-white figure at the top of the hill.

"Excuse me," he called out.

"Can you help me?"

The stripy stranger turned towards him.

"Winter is no place for a hedgehog. You should be in bed."

"Oh no, n-not me! I'm b-big and b-b-brave and I'm staying up to see the winter!" said Little Spike, shivering. "But I've lost my way and now I am c-c-cold and hungry."

"I'm also hungry. Come closer, tiny hedgehog." The creature sneered, revealing a set of sharp teeth.

Suddenly Little Spike did not feel big and brave. He was very afraid. He quickly rolled tightly into a round ball. Only the tip of his nose and front paws peeped out.

A heavy paw prodded him, and suddenly he started to move.

Downhill…

Slowly at first…

Then a little faster…

As he rolled, snow stuck to his bristles.

The faster he rolled, the more snow stuck to him.

Soon Little Spike was hidden in an enormous white snowball.

It rolled *faster* and *faster*,

        getting bigger and bigger…

           All of a sudden, he felt a **THUMP!**

He crashed into a hollow tree stump and the giant
snowball shattered into a thousand pieces. A rather shocked
Little Spike was left curled up in the snow. Twitching his
nose, he snuffled and sniffed. Pine needles and
autumn leaves and…

"Mother!"

Mother Hedgehog opened a sleepy eye.
"Little Spike, where have you been?"

"Oh, Mother, I've seen the winter
and it is no place for a hedgehog.
The freezing north wind whistles,
the river turns to solid ice and
our food is buried beneath a
carpet of snow. I am a
foolish little hoglet."

"Yes, you are. But you
are also my big, brave hoglet
and I love you."

Little Spike stretched and
shook the snow off his bristles.
Squeezing into the cosy nest,
he wriggled and yawned.
"Now Mother, we really
must go to s ... s ... s ... s..."

THE GREAT MEERKAT ESCAPE

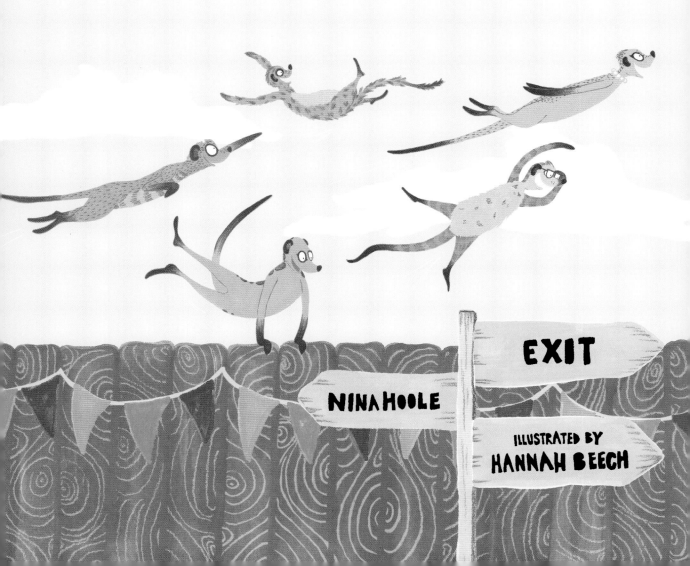

NINA HOOLE

EXIT

ILLUSTRATED BY HANNAH BEECH

"All clear!" squeaked Jimmy.

"Right, gang, does everyone know the plan?" Mac whispered. "Distraction at the front, tower at the back."

A mob of furry heads nodded in agreement.

"Jimmy, you keep lookout. And Scratch?"

A dusty brown face peered up at Mac. "Yes, boss?"

"Keep digging."

"Yes, boss!"

Mac glanced this way and that, waiting for the zoo keeper to walk past.

"Right, everyone into position. And remember: look cute."

Mac gave the signal and the meerkats gathered at the front of the enclosure and put on a show. Handstands, juggling, even a spot of line dancing. Soon all the visitors were pointing and laughing.

Meanwhile, in the shadows at the back, one meerkat climbed onto another's shoulders, forming a tower, until finally they were as tall as the wall. Queenie and Tinker quickly scurried over, just as the tower started to wobble and came tumbling down.

"Did they make it?" hissed Mac.

"Yes, boss," nodded Jimmy from his lookout on the fallen tree.

41

But then a little girl screamed and someone shouted, "One's got loose! There's a meerkat down here. No, two!"

The keeper came running. He picked up Queenie and Tinker by the scruffs of their necks and plopped them back into the enclosure.

"How on earth did they get out?" he muttered as he went back to his rounds.

Queenie and Tinker dusted themselves off and the visitors moved on.

"Hmm…" Mac pondered. "Time to think of a new plan."

Early next morning a visitor swooped down into the enclosure.

"Ah, Magda!" Mac came out of his burrow to welcome her. "Good to see you. What have you brought for us today?"

The magpie often dropped by with useful bits and pieces she'd picked up from around the zoo. In return the meerkats gave her spare tufts of fur to line her nest.

"Well," she chattered, letting a colourful sheet of paper float down from her beak, "I've got a leaflet with a map of the whole zoo, a baby's hat, some old tickets from the zoo train and a broken umbrella."

A furry crowd gathered round to admire the latest treasures.

"Nice," Mac nodded, examining the goods. "Tinker, do you think you can do something with these?"

"Oh yes, boss." Tinker nodded vigorously, sending his glasses sliding down his nose.

"Then take them down to the tunnel, before anyone sees them. And here," Mac said, "is your payment."

Magda hopped over and grasped the fluffy bundles.

"Always a pleasure doing business with you, Mac."

Mac looked on thoughtfully as the magpie flew away. "Hmm … I think I have an idea." He followed Tinker as he dragged the umbrella underground.

Tinker worked all night deep in the tunnel. He pulled the umbrella apart, unpicked the elastic from the baby's hat, rummaged through his dusty shelves for some old knitting needles, and carefully bent the shaft of an old litter-picking stick until it made a perfect square. His eyes felt sore and his paws ached, but by the next morning he had made a trampoline.

"Marvellous," smiled Mac, as two of the babies scrambled on to try it. "Good work, Tinker. Everyone ready, then."

Two meerkats held the trampoline steady while the others formed an orderly line. Queenie was the first to run up.

Ping!

She bounced off the cloth and straight over the wall. One, two, three meerkats followed after her. It was going so well, until suddenly Jimmy squealed, "Stop! Stop!"

MEET ALAN
THE ANTEATER

TO THE MEERKATS

TO THE ZEBRAS

AT
ZOO LATES

The keeper happened to be passing as four meerkats whizzed through the air.

"What on earth!" he exclaimed, as he caught them, one after another. "Flying meerkats?" He dropped them all back into the enclosure and walked away, shaking his head.

"Hmm…" Mac said. "Time to think of a new plan."

A week later, Scratch popped her head out of the entrance to the tunnel.

"It's finished!"

"Marvellous." Mac rubbed his paws together. "Tinker?"

Tinker pushed his glasses back up his nose. "All done. I finished the last coat this morning."

"Excellent. Does everyone remember the plan? Hats down, coats up, tails in."

A huddle of furry heads nodded in agreement.

Ten minutes later a line of very smartly-dressed meerkats hurried down the new tunnel. It came out opposite the monkey house and Scratch quickly led them to the zoo train stop.

Mac handed out the tickets and showed everyone the map.

"We'll meet up at the main exit. Good luck everyone."
The meerkats joined the queue.

"Tickets, please," said the conductor.

Mac kept his head lowered and held out his ticket, but seconds later he heard a familiar voice.

"Hold on a minute. Is that a tail?"

The keeper ran over as Jimmy pulled his tail inside his coat.

"How do they keep getting out?" complained the keeper.

46

"Will you give me a hand getting them back into the enclosure, Fred? Then I'll find the tunnel and block it."

"Hmm…" said Mac, as the meerkats stripped off their disguises. "Scratch, you know what this means?"

"We need another tunnel?"

"Exactly." Mac dipped a paw into his coat pocket and pulled out a bunch of keys. "I found these hanging from the keeper's belt. I think we've got a new plan!"

For two whole weeks the meerkats were on their best behaviour. No escape attempts, no disguises and no hiding. Scratch was hard at work, digging night and day. When the tunnel was finished, they made their final preparations.

The next morning, when the keeper came to check the enclosure, he found the door swinging open and a trail of sand leading towards the lemur walk.

"They've got out again!" he howled, as he ran down the path, looking under bushes and peering into bins.

Back in the latest tunnel, Jimmy squeaked, "He's gone!"

The meerkats quickly made their way down the new burrow, which came out by the drive-through safari. A jeep was pulling a trailer that had been used to deliver food to the antelopes. As the jeep waited for the wire gates to slide open, the gang scrambled up and hid themselves in the trailer.

"Nearly there!" whispered Mac, pulling some hay over himself for camouflage.

"I think I'm going to sneeze!" squeaked Jimmy.

"Just keep calm," hissed Mac.

A siren sounded as the gate opened, making Tinker jump. Bumping down the road to the zoo exit and to freedom, Mac peered up at the large sign:

THANK YOU FOR VISITING. HOPE TO SEE YOU AGAIN SOON!

Mac gave a chuckle as they headed out into the big, wide world. "Let's hope not!"

THE TALE OF THE WINGED LION

Eilidh Mackay

Illustrated by Kate Alizadeh

On a windswept isle, far from land, lived two girls named Gabriela and Sofia. Their father, a merchant who sailed the seas, brought their names from distant shores, carrying them back to the island like treasure. He thought them just about beautiful enough for his precious daughters.

Gabriela and Sofia lived on a small farm with their parents and grandparents. Their father would return from his voyages with colourful trinkets and wondrous tales. While he was gone, every morning their mother would tutor them: letters, numbers and needlework skills. In the afternoon they would bake bread with their grandmother or run wild in the hills surrounding their home.

Some days the girls would spend hours on the high cliffs watching the sea for a sign of their father's boat and his return home.

Gabriela was a storyteller, endlessly recounting the magical tales her father had told her. Sofia would listen in awe as her older sister painted pictures with words.

Sofia's favourite was the tale of the winged lion. In the long days of summer, the girls would travel to the market in the town square once a week. As they trundled along the bumpy road, perched on the back of their grandfather's wooden cart, Gabriela would delight a wide-eyed Sofia with the adventures of the bronze statue that sat atop the fountain in the town square. He was a magnificent creature with fearsome claws and a flowing mane. When the moon was full and the square deserted, the beast would flap his gigantic wings and soar high above the island to wherever people were in trouble. He could speak any language, even that of the most exotic animal.

Gabriela told of the tribe of nomads who were lost in a vicious sandstorm in a distant desert land. The winged lion guided them to safety by whispering in the ears of their camels. When the winged lion foresaw an erupting volcano, he alerted the citizens of the city below to the danger by telling the city's dogs. The city drowned in lava, but every single person escaped.

"Does the lion speak to ... people?" asked Sofia, as the donkey plodded down the rough road.

"When there is terrible danger," Gabriela replied, gravely, "and only to those who truly believe."

"I believe," said Sofia softly. "Do you, Gabriela?"

The weather grew wilder, the days shorter. Weeks went by when Gabriela and Sofia would stay at home, cosy by the fire, instead of travelling to the town. Then one market day, it dawned bright and crisp and their grandfather decided the girls could come with him. Their mother wrapped them up warmly and waved them off.

When they arrived in the town square, their grandfather went about his business: trading bread, cheese and rough cloth woven from sheep's fleece. Gabriela sat on the edge of the fountain, stroking the bronze lion's foot. Sofia found a cousin and they chased birds in the square, shrieking with laughter.

"I believe," Gabriela said quietly, the bronze cold and smooth under her hand.

"I know you do, Gabriela." The voice was low, almost a purr.

Gabriela gazed up at the lion.

"Did you ... speak to me?" she whispered.

"I need your help." The lion's mouth barely moved, his proud head staring across the busy square. "The animals will tell you when it is time."

"Time for what?" Gabriela gasped.

"Time to go home!" Sofia called. "Gabriela! Grandfather says it's time to go home!"

Gabriela gave the winged lion's foot a last rub, then ran across the square to where her grandfather was waiting.

She heard voices everywhere after that. When she fed the chickens they clucked their thanks. As she skipped past the field, the cows mooed in greeting.

"Time to head south!" a flock of geese honked loudly, flying in a perfectly formed v-shape in the darkening sky.

Gabriela was startled, but soon she whispered back to the donkey, the farm cat, a pretty finch. The animals replied, words woven into their brays and mews and tweets.

Gabriela's stories were filled with magical farm creatures. Sofia listened, rapt. She drifted off to sleep and dreamt of talking cats and laughing donkeys.

As winter drew in, the storms began. No one left the farm for weeks, not even to go to market. Their father was expected home soon, as he had been gone for many weeks. One morning, after a terrifying gale, Gabriela overheard her mother and grandparents' whispered conversation.

"He might not make it this time." Her grandfather laid his weathered hand on her mother's shoulder. Gabriela realized that her mother was sobbing.

Without making a sound, she slipped out and ran
to the donkey's shed.

"Something is wrong!" she cried.

"Tonight, when the moon is high, we must go to the
winged lion," the donkey brayed.

Gabriela knew the time had now come.

When the house was still, Gabriela crept from bed. By the
light of the full moon she led the donkey and cart on to
the track and set off for the town.

The town square slumbered. Gabriela leapt from the
cart and ran towards the winged lion. Before she could
speak, she heard his purr, more urgent than before.

"Climb onto my back, Gabriela. There is not much time."

She did as he said, gripping onto his sculpted mane as his huge wings unfurled. They were in the air, Gabriela holding on tightly. His mane felt soft and the beating of his wings was strong and rhythmic.

After a while, Gabriela grew braver and peered downwards. Far beneath them, she could see the ocean, enormous waves catching in the light of the moon.

"Where are we going?" she called, her words disappearing into the black sky.

"To your father!" the lion bellowed. "He is in danger!"

Gabriela felt the winged lion descending.

"Hold on, you will be safe!" the winged lion growled, as the sea thrashed wildly below.

Gabriela saw a boat, illuminated by a moonbeam, being tossed by the waves like a toy.

"That's my father's boat!"

Gabriela screamed as she recognized the figure at the helm. "Father!"

"They are heading into the storm!" The lion's voice was steady above the noise. "They will die unless we can steer them to safety!"

"But how?" Gabriela felt tears on her cheeks.

Through the darkness, something caught her eye — a movement near the boat. A pod of dolphins was leaping through the waves alongside the struggling vessel. With all of her heart, Gabriela willed the dolphins to help her father. Over the raging wind, she heard the winged lion's purr growing louder in her ears.

A moment later, one of the crew pointed to the diving creatures. Gabriela's father wrestled with the wheel, fighting valiantly against the elements.

The dolphins were guiding the boat away from the storm. The winged lion had understood Gabriela and, thanks to him, the gentle creatures of the sea had heard her plea.

All at once, the roaring wind started to subside. The winged lion flew alongside the boat, his mighty wings easily defeating the weakening gusts.

Behind them, Gabriela saw the horizon glow with the rising sun. As the yellow orb appeared in the east, a huge bird swooped by, vast wings held straight and steady as it glided downwards. A yell went up from the deck.

An exhausted sailor had spotted the bird, an albatross.

"They are safe now," the winged lion growled, soaring upwards. "The albatross will take them home."

Gabriela squeezed her eyes closed as the lion's wings beat faster and faster...

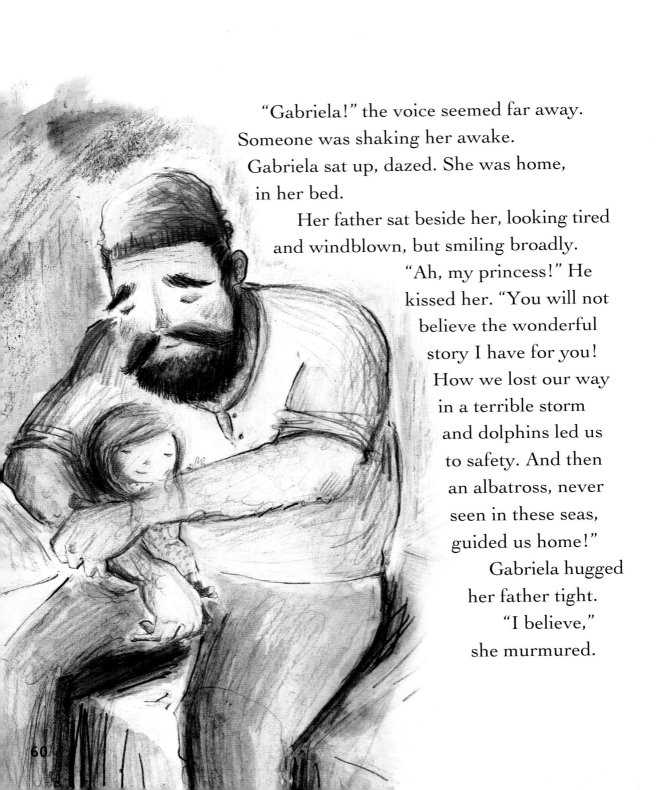

"Gabriela!" the voice seemed far away.
Someone was shaking her awake.
Gabriela sat up, dazed. She was home,
in her bed.

Her father sat beside her, looking tired
and windblown, but smiling broadly.

"Ah, my princess!" He
kissed her. "You will not
believe the wonderful
story I have for you!
How we lost our way
in a terrible storm
and dolphins led us
to safety. And then
an albatross, never
seen in these seas,
guided us home!"

Gabriela hugged
her father tight.
"I believe,"
she murmured.

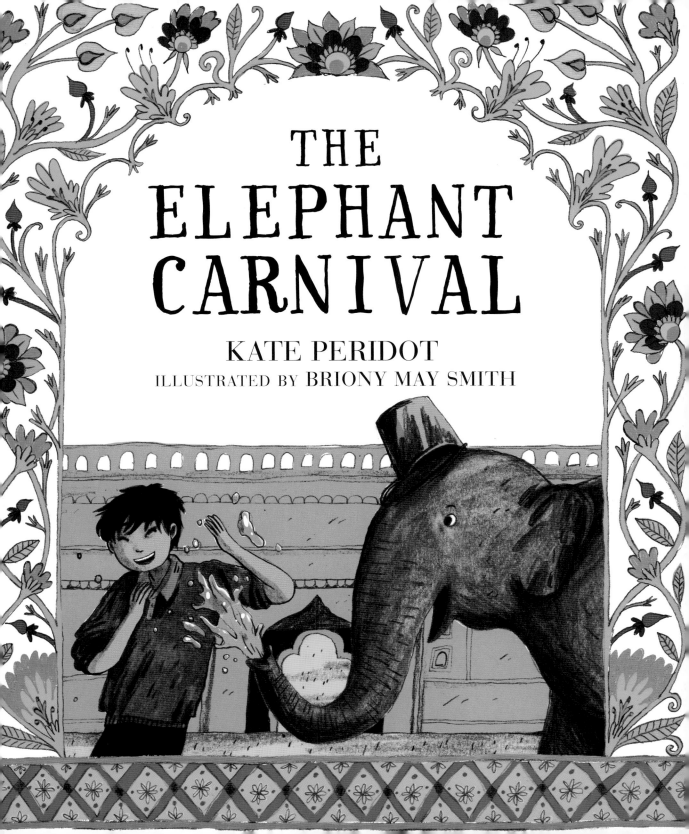

THE ELEPHANT CARNIVAL

KATE PERIDOT

ILLUSTRATED BY BRIONY MAY SMITH

Nandi helped Mata and Pita carry the heavy boxes of carnival clothes and elephant jewellery into the house. In two days' time the Jaipur Elephant Festival would begin. A carnival of beautifully decorated elephants would parade through the streets, followed by three days of music, singing and dancing.

Nandi's pita was a mahout – an elephant keeper – and looked after Kiruba and her calf, Bobo. Kiruba's owner wanted Kiruba to take part in the carnival, and if she won, Nandi's family would get half a bag of gold coins. Nandi knew his mata and pita needed the money to mend their roof before the heavy rains came at the end of the summer.

"Do you think Kiruba will win, Pita?" Nandi asked.

"We'll try our best, but every mahout in Jaipur wants to win."

"We'll watch the parade from Auntie Nina's balcony," said Mata. Nandi groaned. Auntie's balcony was tiny, high up and away from all the fun. He wanted to be down in the street among the thousands of people, or even better, up on Kiruba's big, strong back.

"Pita, why can't I ride on Kiruba with you?"

Pita shook his head. "Only a mahout or an owner is allowed to ride on an elephant in the carnival."

"But I am a mahout! I look after Bobo," Nandi cried. Every day, before and after school, Nandi swept the elephant dung from the yard and gave Bobo peanuts and bananas. He had learnt all the words and hand signals a mahout used and had practised them with Bobo.

"Bobo is too young to be in a carnival," Pita said. "He might get frightened."

A frightened elephant running scared could hurt someone. But Nandi didn't think Bobo would be scared. Bobo had always been a show-off. He was even named after a clown. He loved to play tricks on people. His favourite was putting a bucket of water on his head and squirting anybody who walked by with his trunk.

"Bobo won't get scared," Nandi pleaded.

Pita shook his head. "We must wait until he is older. Bobo will stay here. My decision is final."

Nandi sighed and went over to Bobo, who was resting in the shade of the banyan tree with Kiruba. His head hung low and his trunk was on the ground. Nandi thought Bobo understood a lot of human words. He looked as if he had understood every word Pita had said.

"I know, Bobo. It's not fair," Nandi said, patting him. He pressed his face into Bobo's neck.

Bobo curled his trunk around Nandi's waist and squeezed him affectionately.

"Come on, the river will cheer us up," Nandi said. "Let's have a mud bath." Bobo trumpeted excitedly. For a while, they splashed and swam and forgot about the carnival.

Early on the day of the carnival, Mata prepared colourful paints to decorate Kiruba. She stood still and proud as Mata painted ornate flowers onto her grey hide.

"Can I paint Bobo?" Nandi said. "Then he won't feel so left out."

Mata smiled. "Use up what paint is left. He'll have to stand very still."

Nandi painted Bobo's trunk red, his face white and made huge black circles around Bobo's eyes. He painted juggling balls on his legs and flaming hoops on his back and even found an old red sunhat to put on Bobo's head. "You really are a clown elephant now," laughed Nandi.

Pita came out of the
house dressed in a smart white suit
and a red turban. He placed a beautiful
red silk cloth, embroidered with golden thread
and jewels, over Kiruba's back. Mata looped gold
bracelets with tiny bells around Kiruba's ankles
and placed a triangle of gold cloth, set with tiny
mirrors and glittering stones, on the elephant's head.
"Kiruba, you look
beautiful," Nandi gasped
and Bobo trumpeted in
agreement.

Nandi and Mata
waved goodbye and shouted good
luck as the elephant and her mahout set
off for the town square, where the judging
would take place.

"Quick, wash the paint off your hands and get
dressed! We don't want to miss the announcement
of the winner," said Mata.

Nandi changed into his best clothes and helped
his mother put on her best sari. Then they rushed
out of the door.

Nandi's heart sank when he saw the other elephants in the square. They were all spectacularly dressed and beautifully painted.

"And the winner is …" cried the judge, "… Avani!"

There was a loud cheer from Avani's owner and his mahout's family.

"We didn't win!" cried Nandi.

Mata took Nandi's hand and gave it a squeeze. "Never mind," she said. "It's the taking part that matters. The carnival is about remembering how blessed we are to have these magnificent animals. It's not just about winning."

The elephants began to move into line, ready for the start of the parade. Nandi waved at Pita and tried to hide his disappointment. He really had thought Kiruba would win.

"Let's go to Auntie's now. It's too hot here," Mata said. They made their way through the crowded streets.

"Bobo!" Nandi suddenly cried. "We were in such a rush, I forgot to attach his chain!"

Mata frowned. "We can't leave him loose in the yard. We'll have to go back. Let's hurry or we'll miss the carnival."

As they turned the corner near to home, Nandi and Mata heard laughter. Bobo stood in the middle of the street, surrounded by people. He was tossing his red sunhat into the air and catching it again with his trunk.

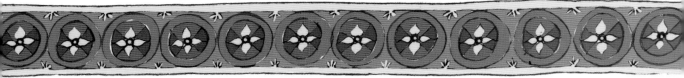

Then he turned around and around on the spot, as fast as he could spin. With his painted clown face he did look funny. Nandi and Mata pushed to the front of the crowd.

"Bobo, what are you doing?" Nandi cried.

Bobo was very pleased to see Nandi. He walked over and hugged him with his trunk, lifting Nandi off his feet. Everybody laughed again.

"Is that your elephant?" a man said. "He knows lots of tricks. I hope he's in the carnival parade."

Then they all heard the sound of the parade drums in the distance.

"We're going to miss it," Mata said, worriedly. The street was now full of people hurrying to see the parade.

Bobo bent down on one knee. Nandi knew what he was thinking and jumped onto his back. "Walk beside us, Mata! Everyone will make way for a painted elephant on carnival day."

When the crowds saw Bobo's painted face and funny hat they cheered and made room for them to pass.

Suddenly, they were through the crowd and in the carnival, marching behind the last of the decorated elephants. Behind them were dancers in lion and leopard costumes and a marching band. They were part of the parade! Bobo marched to the beat of the drums, then stopped to twirl and throw his hat. When Nandi caught it, the crowd cheered.

That evening, Nandi had a lot of explaining to do. Pita was cross until he realized that Kiruba and Bobo's owner had been watching the parade. Everyone had asked him who the little clown elephant belonged to. They wanted to see more of Bobo's tricks and have their pictures taken with the funny elephant.

Bobo's owner asked Nandi
to put on a weekly show in the town square.
When Nandi held out Bobo's red hat at the end
of the show, people filled it with coins. Nandi had to
give half of the money to Bobo's owner, but Pita got
to keep the other half. Soon he had enough to fix the roof.
And of course from the day of the carnival onwards, Nandi
always made sure Bobo got plenty of his favourite peanuts.

a Pile of Panda

JULIE INNES
ILLUSTRATED BY RACHEL STUBBS

Dotty had three wishes. What should she wish for? She had so many ideas… Dotty had to think about this carefully. She made a list of the things she wanted most of all:

A cute and cuddly plaything she could dress up.

A wise and kind friend to share her secrets.

To be so famous everyone would know her name.

It was obvious. With one clever wish she could have all these things. Dotty thought hard, then closed her eyes and made a wish. She wished for …

a real, live panda!

She couldn't quite believe her eyes. There he was, a whole pile of panda, at the end of her bed.

I could dress him in a sunhat, thought Dotty.

Pandas are known for their wisdom and sensitivity, too.

Everyone will say, "Have you heard? Dotty's best friend is a real, live panda!" They'll really know who I am.

But Panda didn't look quite as cute and cuddly as Dotty had imagined.

She cleaned him up, borrowed some clothes that just about fit, and wheeled him out to the playground.

He broke the swing.

He was too lazy to climb the slide.

The roundabout was a complete disaster.

So Panda wasn't the perfect plaything after all. Even so, Dotty was sure that he would be a great friend.

She invited Panda to tea, so that they could discuss Dotty's deepest, darkest secrets. She made a civilized spread of peanut butter sandwiches, custard creams and pink milk.

But Panda didn't listen! He was more interested in the wicker chair. So much so, he swallowed it whole. Then he sat there, burping and picking his teeth with a dirty claw.

So he wasn't cute and he was a terrible friend.

No one else liked Panda either.
They ran and hid whenever he was around. Dotty was definitely famous, but for the wrong reason!

Dotty decided he had to go. He wasn't what she had wished for.

It wasn't going to be easy to get rid of him. No one else wanted him. She needed a plan.

First she tried Plan A. It took rather a lot of tape, but Dotty eventually managed to wrap Panda up and drag him to the Post Office. Unfortunately her piggy bank didn't cover the postage to China.

So she tried Plan B. Dotty thought that perhaps he would be happier with his own kind. The zoo would love to have him.

It wasn't long before the zoo keepers sent him back, with a report of inappropriate behaviour and poor personal hygiene.

She even considered a desperate Plan C. Dotty remembered a story about how to turn a frog into a prince… She let Panda sleep on her pillow and eat from her plate.

But a kiss … not even Dotty had the courage to do that.

Dotty had run out of plans.

There was only one thing for it. She would have to use her precious second wish to send Panda back where he came from.

She shut her eyes … and he was gone!

Now, I can't exactly say that Dotty missed Panda. But she did feel life was lacking a certain something, and she did have one last wish…

What harm could a sweet little bunny do, after all?

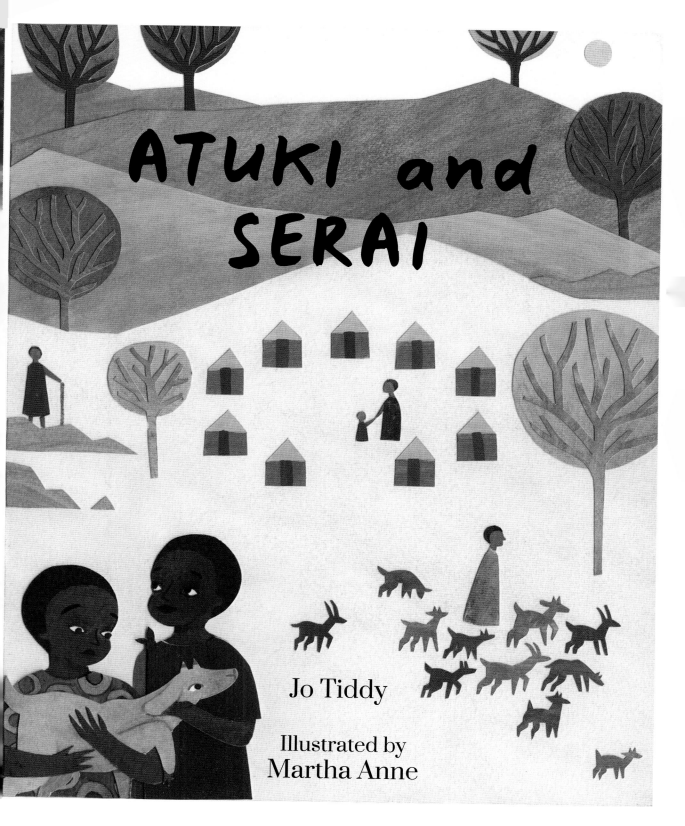

ATUKI and SERAI

Jo Tiddy

Illustrated by
Martha Anne

When Atuki turns six, her mother gives her a bright necklace of ostrich-shell beads and a small goat. The goat is brown and black, with a tiny voice that goes, "Maa, maa."

Atuki loves her. "I shall call her Serai," she says. "I shall keep her safe."

Mother says, "You are old enough to take Serai out with the other children now, but stay close to them."

The village has many goats. Every day the children walk a long way in the afternoon heat, their goats nibbling on branches and buds the whole time. Atuki looks at the other goats. One has a bell that jangles merrily. She thinks Serai might like a bell.

"Don't be silly," says one of the bigger children, and they all laugh.

"Why do some goats have bells?" Atuki asks Mother.

"They are the leaders, the wise goats. Other goats will follow them. The bell means they can always be found, even if they have drifted a long way through the bush."

"Can I have a bell for Serai?"

Mother laughs. "She's too little and not very clever yet. She has much to learn. You will have to teach her."

As the sun sinks in the sky, Atuki leads Serai into the thick thorn boma that will keep the goats safe all night.

Serai does not want to go in. She makes a fuss. "Maa, maa," she bleats.

"Stop, Serai," says Atuki. "Chui, the leopard, is ever hungry. His favourite dinner is goat. Go inside so you can sleep safely. He can't get through the tall thorns."

Every day after lessons, Atuki goes out with Serai into the bush. They play at climbing the rocks on the kopje, until Serai can climb faster than any other goat. They play hide-and-seek, and soon Serai can hide behind the smallest tree and not be seen.

Atuki thinks that maybe now Serai could have a bell.

"She has much more to learn. You will have to teach her," say the other children, laughing.

Some days the well is dry and Atuki has to fetch water. Serai is thirsty, and she bounces down towards the riverbank.

"Stop, Serai," says Atuki. "See that log floating in the water? That is Mamba, the crocodile. His teeth are very sharp. He is waiting for careless goats to come too close. Better to drink from that puddle over there."

In time the rains come. Every day dark clouds billow up
on the horizon, and spears of rain pour down, turning
the tracks into streams.

Serai sees a dark line in the dirt and trots over to take
a closer look.

"Stop, Serai," says Atuki. "Those are the siafu, an army of
ants, ever marching, ever hungry. They will nip if you tread
on them." The ants swirl around, waving their sharp pincers.

When they get home Mother puts piles of ash around
the boma to keep the ants away.

After the rains have gone, the grass grows tall and green. Serai likes to hide in it, keeping very quiet.

"Stop, Serai," says Atuki, banging a tin can as she walks. "Nyoka, the snake, has a sharp bite. He likes to hide in the long grass, but he is more afraid of you than you are of him. You need to let him know you are coming so he can slide away."

As the land heats up, the big herds of game pass through, following the growth of the grass. Atuki and Serai look out over the plains. The animals seem small and far away. There is one, closer: big and black. Serai bounds off to take a closer look.

"Stop, Serai," yells Atuki. "That is Nyati, the buffalo. He is very bad-tempered. You need to keep out of his way." Nyati has sweeping horns. A little white bird sits on his back picking at ticks. "The bird helps him," adds Atuki. "He is his only friend."

Atuki thinks that now Serai must have learned enough to have a bell.

"Not yet," says Mother. "She has much more to learn. You will have to teach her."

One day Atuki and Serai go a long way into the bush. They don't notice the time. There are so many things to look at: the hyraxes sunning themselves on the rocks, the weaver birds building houses in the thorn trees.

Suddenly Atuki notices that the sun has sunk to the horizon. She stops and listens. She can't hear anything; no bells, no goats, no children's voices.

Darkness comes suddenly and Atuki is worried that she is lost. Serai keeps trotting happily and Atuki runs to keep up. She catches her foot in an anthole and falls. When she tries to stand, she finds she cannot.

"Stop, Serai," she wails. "I've hurt my leg." Serai stops, turns back to Atuki and nuzzles her with her little brown nose.

In the darkness they hear a loud chuckle, coming closer.

"Hush, Serai," says Atuki in a little voice. "That is Fisi, the hyena. He is big and strong and cruel. I am frightened." A shape looms out of the darkness, and they hear the chuckle again.

Serai turns and runs through the bush. She bleats very loudly, making as much noise as possible. Fisi turns to follow her. Atuki can hear Serai getting fainter and fainter. All she can do is wait.

Sometime later there is the sound of many people coming through the bush. The cattle dogs are with them, snarling at the dark. Torches flicker like stars as people call out, "Atuki, Atuki!" She is so happy to see them that she forgets her fear and the pain in her leg.

Mother is cross and happy at the same time. "Silly girl," she says, "staying out so late!"

But Atuki is crying. "I have lost Serai," she sobs. "She led Fisi away."

Atuki's mother smiles at her small daughter.

"She is safe. She came back to the village and made so much noise that she woke us all up. She's a very clever goat. Look!"

She steps to one side, and there is Serai, small and brown and black. Around her neck is a lovely jangly bell.

LINDSAY LITTLESON

Up In the Trees IS NOT FOR Me!

Illustrated by FAYE BRADLEY

"No way am I climbing up that tree," said Max.
"It's way too high and I'm way too wee. Up in the trees is not for me!"

"Don't be silly, Max," scolded Mum. "Spider monkeys love to climb. It's what we do best. Look!"

She pointed up in the trees where Max's whole family were scrambling, leaping and clambering up and up through the leafy branches. They pulled juicy purple fruit from the trees and crammed it in their mouths, spitting juice as they chattered. Old Grandpa Bob crouched high on a sturdy branch of the giant kapok tree. He loudly barked warnings when the younger, sillier monkeys climbed too high, where the branches were thin and breakable, or if they strayed too far from the group.

Max's cousin, Fern, was climbing higher and faster than any of the other spider monkeys. She was as graceful as a dancer and as agile as an acrobat. She swung happily from branch to branch, shrieking with joy. "Max, look at me! Look at me! I'm high in the sky!"

"Show off!" muttered Max, crossly, as he crouched among the leaf litter on the forest floor.

He poked his fingers in some spongy
moss and surprised a tree frog. It jumped high
in the air, then sprang onto a tree trunk and bounced
up, up and up. Max sighed. Even the rainforest frogs
loved to climb. He was the odd one out.

"Come on, Max," said Mum, kindly. "Why don't you hold
onto me and we'll go for a swing together like we used to do when
you were very small? You'll be safe on my back."

"No way am I doing that," grumbled Max. "Everyone will
laugh at me. I'm not a baby, I'm just too little to climb trees yet.
I shall sit down here and wait until I am a bit taller. Up in
the trees is not for me!" And he turned his back on Mum and
scrabbled in the dead leaves, pretending he was looking for nuts.

"Well, I'm going for a climb in the trees," said Mum. "I like
it up in the canopy where the sun glitters on the wet leaves and
warms my fur … and where the fruit grows ripe and juicy."

Mum scrambled up the vast twisted trunk of the kapok tree.
Max watched in wonder as she swung through the branches,
her long, gangly arms, legs and tail looping and twisting in a
swirl of velvet fur. She grew smaller as she moved further and
further up the giant tree and further away from him.

"That looks scary and dangerous," Max decided. "The ground
is a much better, safer place to be. Up in the trees is definitely
not for me."

He sniffed around again in the leaf litter, but couldn't find anything tasty to eat. High in the canopy he could hear his family. Branches creaked as spider monkeys swung from tree to tree. Fern screeched her happy screech, Mum chattered loudly to his aunts about which trees had the ripest fruit and Grandpa Bob grumbled noisily about his sore joints.

Max sighed. It was lonely down on the forest floor. The insects were no fun. They crawled or scuttled or slithered away every time he came near. A beautiful blue morpho butterfly rested for a moment on Max's furry arm and then fluttered silently up towards the treetops, its lovely wings shimmering.

Max studied the strong and sturdy kapok tree. It looked as if it had been standing for a thousand years. He reached out a hand and stroked the bark. Could he climb it? Could he? He gripped the trunk with both hands and pulled himself up a little way. Then a little further… Max looked down at the ground. It looked far away. He quickly slid back down the rough trunk.

"No way am I climbing up that tree," said Max firmly to himself. "It's way too high and I'm way too wee. Up in the trees is not for me!"

He was hungry and he could smell juicy berries high above him. He didn't want to eat nuts. No way was he going to eat bugs. Maybe he should call Mum. She would bring him some fruit. Just as he opened his mouth to yell, he suddenly froze…

Padding silently towards Max through the
trees was a huge, spotted jaguar. His eyes were
fixed on Max. He had enormous velvety paws, long
white whiskers and gleaming orange eyes.

Max gulped. He turned and scurried towards
the kapok tree.

Up he climbed. Up, up and up. The jaguar could climb a tree, but not as fast and not as high as a spider monkey. Not as fast and not as high as Max!

Max swung and clambered, leapt and scrambled, hand over hand, using his long tail and gangly limbs to climb further and further in the forest canopy. At last he stopped. He looked down and saw the jaguar padding silently back into the forest.

Max looked around him. No monkeys were climbing or swinging. They were crouched in the treetops, eyes wide with amazement, looking at Max. And then they cheered and clapped and patted him on the back. Max was up in the trees, where spider monkeys belong.

Max sighed happily as he looked at his family gathered around him. He could see juicy purple fruit growing in fat clusters and the sunlight was warming his fur. Mum gave him a big hug. "What do you think, Max? Do you like climbing after all?"

Max grinned a big happy grin. "No way am I climbing down that tree," he said firmly. "The forest floor's too scary and I'm way too wee. Down on the ground is not for me!"

BASIL THE BRAVE

ALICE WESTLAKE

ILLUSTRATED BY EMMA COLLINS

More than anything, Basil wanted to fly. Every day he looked out of the crumbling belfry, across the green-gold common, and watched the kites as they dipped and dived and scurried and soared. One moment they skimmed the lake so low that, when they rose up again, their bellies were jewelled with water. The next moment they looped the loop and performed all manner of death-defying feats.

Basil longed to join them, to plunge nose-first towards the ground like a meteor and at the very last moment flick up and away into the sky. He looked at his family, hanging folded up like umbrellas from their sleepy perch, and wondered what it would be like to fly with the kites in the bright sunshine.

Then one day the kites were gone. Children's laughter no longer floated up from the common. Only the distant strains of the school bell could be heard on the wind. There was a chill in the air and the leaves started to turn red and gold, umber and speckled brown. Basil watched them whisking and wheeling, whipped by the wind, and wished that he could join them.

But each evening when dusk fell, Basil didn't feel so brave any more. His family woke up, stretched their crumpled wings, and prepared to fly. Basil shrank from the ledge, mumbling into his fur that he wasn't coming tonight.

"It's too cold," he complained one night.

"Nonsense!" said his mother. "It's going to get a lot colder than this. Why, winter's hardly begun."

"But I can't fly very well," said Basil another time. "What if I get it all wrong?"

"Don't worry," said his father. "Everyone makes mistakes at first. You just need to take the plunge and try. You might catch a juicy spider."

"I don't even like eating spiders," Basil protested. "Their legs get tangled up in my whiskers."

"What rot!" scoffed his grandfather, running a claw through his own luxuriant grey whiskers.

One gloomy night, Basil hung back as one by one the others spread their leathery wings and sailed off into the night sky. The last to leave the perch was his grandmother. Pausing on the ledge, she turned and looked at Basil thoughtfully.

"Why don't you tell me what's really wrong?" she asked gently. "Why don't you want to fly?"

And Basil said, in a very tiny voice, "I'm scared of what might happen to me out there."

"Look down at the village," said his grandmother. "What do you see?"

"Well … I can see houses with bright windows, and a string of streetlights like a chain of stars, and—"

"Yes?"

"And here and there I can see a funny round glow … and one of them is moving…"

Basil's grandmother smiled. "Those round glows are pumpkins," she said. "Tonight is Halloween. The perfect night for a baby bat to make his first leap. Come on!"

And she unfurled her old black parachute and swooped down from the ledge and out of sight.

Basil hung there, thinking about what his grandmother had said. It did look rather enticing down in the village, with the streetlights winking and the candles flickering, and the squares of light falling onto the pavement from each window.

Squeezing his eyes shut,
he half-flew, half-fell off the ledge and briefly plummeted,
before he spread his small wings and caught the breeze.

It felt … fine.

The wind was cool under his wings and the sounds
and smells of the night were breathtaking. Basil wasn't sure
if he was terrified or thrilled.

He curled down towards the village, flying above the rooftops.
The occasional plume of smoke rose from a chimney.
It wasn't so bad outside the
belfry after all.

Suddenly he heard a hoot. He turned and saw a huge pair of amber eyes in the blackness. Basil tumbled through the air in fright, plunging headlong into the road.

He perched on the dark pavement, trembling, listening to the owl's distant hoots as it flew away. Up the street, a group of children were carrying a pumpkin with a guttering candle inside. They were dressed in strange costumes, some as witches, some as ghosts, and one as a skeleton with bones that glowed in the dark. Basil swooped over to them and nestled inside the hood of the smallest witch. It made the perfect hiding place. It was warm and cosy, and no one could see him in the folds of her black cloak. The smell of candle wax blended with the sweet smell of their Halloween treats – white chocolate spiders, toffee trolls and phizzing wizards.

The children went from house to house, giggling shyly and pushing each other forward to knock on the doors, piling sweets into a tin. Basil liked them immediately.

At one house, they knocked on the door and when it opened, cried, **"TRICK OR TREAT!"**

A man glared at them from the doorstep.

"What's the trick?" he said, rudely.

The children looked at each other, baffled.

"You haven't got one, have you?" he demanded. "You haven't even got a trick! You just want chocolate!"

The children didn't know what to say, and began to back away from the man, tripping over each other's cloaks in their haste.

Suddenly Basil knew what he had to do. He flew out of the little girl's hood, straight towards the man's face. He swooped round in three great circles and dived back into the hood again.

"WAAAAAARRGGGHHHHH! A BAT! A BAT! IT'S A BAT!" screamed everyone.

The children started shaking the little girl's hood.

"Stop! Stop, you'll hurt it!" the little girl cried.

The man picked up a huge broom and began bashing everything in sight. The boy dropped the pumpkin and the candle went out. In the confusion, Basil flitted away to the safety of a nearby tree.

Only the little girl saw him go. "Fly away, little bat!" she cried, staring after him into the darkness.

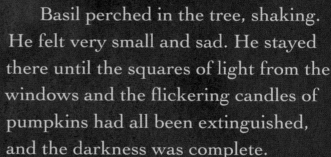

Basil perched in the tree, shaking. He felt very small and sad. He stayed there until the squares of light from the windows and the flickering candles of pumpkins had all been extinguished, and the darkness was complete.

"I knew I should never have left home," he thought, miserably.

Beside the tree, a stream burbled. Moonlight flickered on its surface, broken into a thousand pieces by the rippling water. In its silver light, Basil watched moths darting to and fro. His tummy rumbled with hunger, but he was too frightened to move. Then in the water he saw something else – it looked like a small black kite.

It was hanging dejectedly, caught on a branch. Cautiously, Basil flapped over to it. The kite fluttered too. He stretched out a wing and the kite reached tentatively back. With a start, he realized it was his reflection!

"I really am a kite!" sang Basil, and he turned a triple somersault in surprise. Then he swooped up and down the length of the stream, chasing moths in delight.

He came back to rest in the tree. All he could see were the shapes of branches moving blackly against the velvet sky. But he wasn't scared. Everything was peaceful and still. The sharp edges of the houses were softened by the outlines of trees. The blanket of night was draped over everything.

Basil's tummy rumbled loudly in the silence.
He made his way over to where the children had
dropped their tin of Halloween spoils. Toffee trolls
and phizzing wizards lay strewn across the path,
and oh, white chocolate spiders! Basil lost himself
in a chocolatey, spidery dream...

Suddenly there was a flurry of feathers. An owl
with amber eyes was swooping down towards him.
Basil's heart stopped. The owl landed on the path and
stretched out a huge talon. Basil couldn't move for fear.

"Hello, little chap," said the owl, cheerfully.
"White chocolate spiders! Aren't they scrummy?"

Soon Basil was so busy chatting, he didn't notice
his grandmother gliding silently towards them.

"Basil!" she said. "You've got chocolate all over
your whiskers!"

"Grandma! I've had such an adventure!" he
said happily.

"I've met an owl, and I like eating spiders now –
chocolate ones, anyway – and … and I want to do it
all again tomorrow night!"

"Well, in that case," his grandmother smiled,
"it's time I was getting you home to bed."

And they flew off together over the green-gold
common, pink in the morning's first rays.